Ribbon's Way

Sarah E. Turner

sononis PRESS

Acknowledgements

Ribbon's Way is based on my scientific field studies of monkeys in Japan. My deepest thanks to the Nobuhara and Nakahashi families for permission to conduct research at the Awajishima Monkey Center, and to Masayuki Nakamichi, Kosaku and Keiko Okada, and Fumiaki and Hiroko Taniguchi for making my research in Japan possible. I am very grateful to so many people in Canada and Japan for supporting my research—thanks to all of you, especially my PhD advisor, Linda Fedigan; my husband, Damon Matthews; and all the alloparents for childcare help, especially Kate Wyatt. My research has been funded over the years by the following organizations: the Leakey Foundation, an Izaak Walton Killam Memorial Scholarship, the Animal Behavior Society, the Province of Alberta, the University of Calgary, the U of C Department of Anthropology, Global Forest Science, the University of Victoria, the UVic Department of Anthropology, the UVic Centre for Asia Pacific Initiatives, and NSERC.

Thanks to Diane Morriss, Jim Brennan, Dawn Loewen, and Laura Peetoom for their help in realizing *Ribbon's Way*. Linda Fedigan, Damon Matthews, Kathleen Matthews, Shea Turner-Matthews, Molly, Kate, Nancy and Bob Turner, and Susan Wendell commented on drafts of the book. Thank you!

Text and photography copyright © 2012 by Sarah E. Turner

Library and Archives Canada Cataloguing in Publication

Turner, Sarah Elizabeth, 1975-
   Ribbon's way / Sarah Turner.

ISBN 978-1-55039-200-5

   1. Japanese macaque--Juvenile literature. 2. Social behavior in animals--Juvenile literature. I. Title.

QL737.P93T873 2012   j599.8'644   C2012-901961-5

Sono Nis Press most gratefully acknowledges support for our publishing program provided by the Government of Canada through the Canada Book Fund and the Canada Council for the Arts, and by the Province of British Columbia through the British Columbia Arts Council and the Book Publishing Tax Credit, Ministry of Provincial Revenue.

All photography by Sarah Turner, except the photo of Ribbon learning to hop (p. 18), by Hisami Nobuhara, used with permission.

Three of the photos in *Ribbon's Way* were published simultaneously in the *American Journal of Primatology*: DOI 10.1002/ajp.22029.

Edited by Dawn Loewen and Laura Peetoom
Proofread by Audrey McClellan
Cover and interior design by Jim Brennan

Published by
SONO NIS PRESS
Box 160
Winlaw, BC V0G 2J0
1-800-370-5228
books@sononis.com
www.sononis.com

Distributed in the U.S. by
Orca Book Publishers
Box 468
Custer, WA 98240-0468
1-800-210-5277

Printed and bound in Canada by Houghton Boston Printers.
Printed on acid-free paper that is forest friendly (100% post-consumer recycled paper) and has been processed chlorine free.

The Canada Council | Le Conseil des Arts
for the Arts | du Canada

*for Jane and Shea
and in memory of Mr. Minoru Nakahashi,
founder of the Awaji Island Monkey Center*

"Mommy! There's a new baby! Latie had her baby!" The little girl ran up, breathless. Together they quietly approached the mother monkey. A tiny face could just be seen in the tight snuggle of Latie's arms.

"So cute. So tiny. Like a little gift. Let's call her Ribbon." The girl's mother gave Latie a piece of fruit.

As the mother monkey reached to take the treat, the little girl and her mother got a better look at baby Ribbon.

"Oh, no!" cried the little girl.

The baby monkey did not have any hands. Her arms ended in little round points. Her feet looked strange and small and twisted.

"Ribbon won't be able to hold on to her mommy," the little girl said sadly.

As if in answer, Latie wrapped her arm around the tiny new baby. Then she climbed a nearby tree, holding Ribbon close and safe.

"I guess they will do it their own way," said the little girl's mother as they walked back to the Monkey Center.

Ribbon felt warm in her mother's arms. Her bright eyes watched everything happening around her.

For many days Ribbon watched and nursed. Her mother held her close. Sometimes, if Latie's arms grew tired, she lay down to nurse her baby. Sometimes she leaned against a rock or a tree, gently pressing baby Ribbon in between. Snug between the rock and her mother, Ribbon closed her eyes, drank her mother's milk, and enjoyed the gentle ocean breeze.

"I've never seen a mommy monkey nurse her baby like that before," smiled the little girl.

As Ribbon grew bigger and stronger, she could straighten her back and hold herself up to nurse. But her mother still groomed her, held her most of the time, and carried her everywhere.

"Look at that poor little thing!" exclaimed a tourist, watching Ribbon practise her first movements on her own.

Ribbon didn't understand, and she ignored the tourists anyway. She concentrated on bunching up her back legs, crouching on her elbows, and launching herself forward. The first time, she landed on her nose and squeaked loudly.

Kee! Kee! Kee!

Latie ran over from where she was grooming with one of the aunties. She scooped Ribbon up and carried her away for some milk.

Soon, other baby monkeys came over to where they were sitting, and Ribbon's cousin Peter reached out and touched her arm. Peter and the other baby monkeys climbed around in the low branches, and Ribbon wiggled out from under her mother's arm and watched. Peter jumped down onto Ribbon in a playful wrestle. Ribbon bunched up her back legs, crouched on her elbows, launched herself forward…and landed on Peter! Peter leaped up and they rolled around together making monkey play-faces.

Ribbon soon became very good at her forward jumping movements, landing on all fours like a little grasshopper.

"I have never seen a baby monkey move that way!" said the little girl one morning.

"I guess Ribbon has learned to walk her own way," said her mother.

"It's kind of a slow way," the little girl said doubtfully. "How will she keep up with the others when Latie stops carrying her?"

Ribbon felt good moving around and playing in her own way, but it *was* hard to keep up with the other baby monkeys, especially when they played in the branches. She launched herself at the low boughs and got her arm hooked over a branch. But, struggle as she might, she could not get any higher and soon fell back down.

Kee! Kee! she called after the others in frustration. Her mother came over and groomed Ribbon with reassuring hands.

A few days later, as Ribbon was following behind a group of baby monkeys, she hopped forward…and landed only on her back legs! She kept hopping and hopping. Although she soon fell on her elbows again, she had felt the exciting speed of this new kind of movement.

Over the months that followed, Ribbon's legs grew stronger, and her balance got better. Soon she was on two legs everywhere she went. And as Ribbon grew up, her own special sideways hop-run let her race down the slopes as fast as anyone!

Ribbon still wanted very badly to explore the monkey playground of arching and forked branches. Climbing was hard, but Ribbon did not give up.

As more months passed, Ribbon learned that she could get up most trees with a little squeezing and pinching of her arms and legs. She did fall once in a while. But she felt so good and natural in the branches that she always picked herself up and climbed again, slowly, in her own way.

Each year that went by, Ribbon grew bigger and stronger. She used her feet for things other monkeys did with their hands, like pounding the ground to scare up tasty insects. When the other monkeys played in the water with their hands, Ribbon would sit and enjoy the cool water on her feet.

Ribbon did lots of things that the other monkeys didn't. When she felt tired, she liked to lean against a tree trunk, resting her legs and arms. Sometimes she used a railing at the Monkey Center for support when walking. And she found creative ways to get at an itch!

Ribbon still loved to play with the other young monkeys, but now they spent less time romping about. Instead, they sat in the shade, grooming each other.

One afternoon, Ribbon's cousin Momoko groomed Ribbon's back and her arms and legs and her little rounded feet. Ribbon closed her eyes.

Then it was her turn to groom. Using her elbows, she parted the hair on her cousin's back, then used her mouth to pick out bits from Momoko's hair. Momoko relaxed and closed her eyes.

After a while Ribbon wandered away and found her own place to hang out.

"Look at that silly monkey!" laughed a tourist.

Ribbon glanced over for only a second before closing her eyes for a nap of her own.

The sun sank low behind the green hills. Ribbon woke to the sound of people bringing out the evening food for the monkeys. She jumped up and ran to the Monkey Center. Monkeys were everywhere, picking up grain with their nimble fingers and stuffing their cheek pouches as fast as they could.

Ribbon bent over and used her elbows to push the grain into a pile. Then she ate quickly from the pile, filling up her own cheek pouches with grain for later. The girl, who like Ribbon had grown older and taller, walked by and slipped Ribbon a piece of apple. Ribbon stuffed that into her cheek pouch too. When two young monkeys tried to take her treat, she opened her mouth wide, showing all her teeth, and chased them around the Monkey Center.

But soon there was a treat for everyone! After the monkeys had finished the grain, the girl and her father opened big boxes of oranges and threw them for the monkeys. There was a crazy scramble as all the monkeys rushed to get one.

Ribbon pushed her way to the middle of the rumpus and pounced on a big, juicy one. The girl and her father watched as Ribbon pressed the orange between her arms. She hopped up the slope as fast as she could and, with one big leap, landed on top of a wooden umbrella, away from the others. Soon all was quiet as each monkey found a place to enjoy the fruit.

The next day, Ribbon was grooming with her family while the girl and her mother watched.

"Remember when Ribbon was a tiny baby, Mom? Now she is five years old. Soon she might have a baby of her own."

One of the tourists overheard the girl and asked, with a worried look, "How could *that* monkey look after a baby?"

The girl and her mother smiled at each other. "Don't worry," they said. "Ribbon will figure it out, her own way."

And she did!

More About Ribbon

- Ribbon is a real monkey. She was born in 2001 in the forest near the Awaji Island Monkey Center, in southeastern Japan.
- Ribbon and the other monkeys in this story are Japanese macaques (muh-KACKS), sometimes called snow monkeys.
- Wild Japanese macaques are found only in Japan.
- Ribbon lives with about 200 other Japanese macaques in the forests around the Awaji Island Monkey Center.
- About one out of every six monkeys at the Awaji Island Monkey Center is born with limb malformations, such as bent or absent fingers and toes. Some, like Ribbon, have malformations that cause extensive physical disabilities.
- No one knows exactly why this is happening, but it may be related to pesticides or genetics or both.
- Disabled monkeys live in the group and are treated more or less the same way as other monkeys.
- Baby monkeys without disabilities are able to hold on to their mothers when they are born or very soon after.
- Like Latie, mother monkeys who have disabled babies give those babies extra care, carrying them with an arm and holding them up to nurse.

- Ribbon gave birth to her first baby in 2010. She looked after her baby well. She carried him while walking on her two legs, and he held on to her with his hands.

- Female Japanese macaques with disabilities don't necessarily have babies with disabilities, but sometimes they do, and even so, they figure out ways of carrying and caring for them.

- Female Japanese macaques have a strict dominance hierarchy. That means that from very early on they learn which monkeys can boss them around and which ones they can boss around, and usually it doesn't change much throughout their lives.

- Ribbon was born into a high-ranking family, so she was able to chase off lower-ranking monkeys.

RIBBON'S FOREST WORLD

Ribbon and the other monkeys at the Monkey Center share their forest home with many creatures. Some, like the Japanese sika deer, are quite common and easy to observe. Others, like the frogs on the forest floor, are so well camouflaged that it takes a careful eye to spot them. Can you find the 24 creatures in the photos on these pages? Turn to the next page for answers.

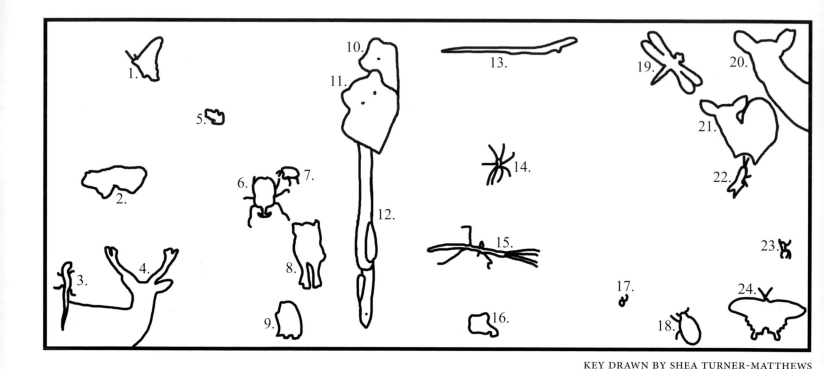

KEY DRAWN BY SHEA TURNER-MATTHEWS

1. Common bluebottle butterfly
2. Japanese western common toad
3. Japanese five-lined skink
4. Adult male sika deer
5. Tago's brown frog
6. Male rhinoceros beetle
7. Japanese drone scarab beetle
8. Young wild boar

9. Japanese marten
10. Baby tanuki raccoon-dog
11. Baby tanuki raccoon-dog
12. Japanese four-lined snake
13. Japanese grass lizard
14. Huntsman spider
15. Japanese stick insect
16. Tago's brown frog

17. Dew-drop spider
18. Japanese drone scarab beetle
19. Wandering glider dragonfly
20. Adult female sika deer
21. Young sika deer
22. Butterbur grasshopper
23. Satsuma trick spider
24. Red Helen swallowtail butterfly

Author's Note

I have known Ribbon since the first day her mother carried her down to the Awaji Island Monkey Center as a newborn baby. I was a master's student, and Ribbon's mother was one of the monkeys I was studying. When Ribbon was born, I would follow them both, writing down all the things that they did. Later, when I went back to the Monkey Center for my PhD work, Ribbon was again one of the monkeys I studied, and I watched her grow into an adult. Ribbon and the other monkeys at the Monkey Center are so used to people being around that they don't seem to care much what we do—unless there is food involved! The monkeys especially trust the owners of the Monkey Center: Mr. Toshikazu Nobuhara, Mrs. Hisami Nobuhara, and their daughter, Saki-chan. Saki-chan has a unique closeness with the monkeys of Awajishima, having grown up with them her whole life.

Ribbon's Way is a true story, but sometimes I used what I know about other Japanese macaques to fill in more details of Ribbon's life. Also, baby monkeys grow up fast, and they don't wait around for you to take their picture! So a few of the photos in this book are of other baby monkeys with disabilities like Ribbon's.

You can learn more about the monkeys at the Awaji Island Monkey Center by reading my first book, *The Littlest Monkey*. And if you ever travel to Japan, you can visit them yourself!

Also by Sarah E. Turner

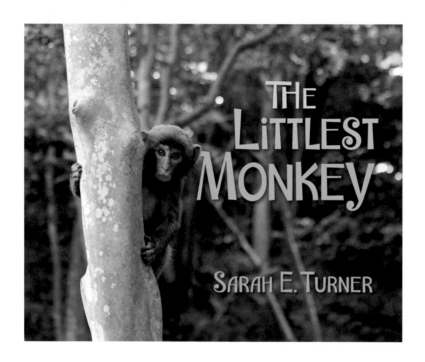

The Littlest Monkey

"Tombo sees a tiny face snuggled up to his mother! The new baby monkey opens her eyes and looks at him just before his mother pushes him gently but firmly away."

Primatologist Sarah Turner's compelling photographs and simple text illuminate every page as she shares this universal tale about growing up, moving over, and finding our way in the world.

ISBN 978-1-55039-174-9 • 9" x 7.5" • 32 pages • paper • $9.95